This book belongs to

....

....

GROSSET & DUNLAP
Published by the Penguin Group
Penguin Group (USA) Inc., 375 Hudson Street, New York, New York 10014, U.S.A.
Penguin Group (Canada), 10 Alcorn Avenue, Toronto, Ontario M4V 3B2, Canada
(a division of Pearson Penguin Canada Inc.)
Penguin Books Ltd, 80 Strand, London WC2R 0RL, England
Penguin Ireland, 25 St Stephen's Green, Dublin 2, Ireland
(a division of Penguin Books Ltd)
Penguin Group (Australia), 250 Camberwell Road, Camberwell, Victoria 3124, Australia
(a division of Pearson Australia Group Pty Ltd)
Penguin Books India Pvt Ltd, 11 Community Centre, Panchsheel Park, New Delhi–110 017, India
Penguin Group (NZ), Cnr Airborne and Rosedale Roads, Albany, Auckland 1310, New Zealand
(a division of Pearson New Zealand Ltd)
Penguin Books (South Africa) (Pty) Ltd, 24 Sturdee Avenue, Rosebank, Johannesburg 2196, South Africa

Penguin Books Ltd, Registered Offices:
80 Strand, London WC2R 0RL, England

First published in the United States 2005
by Grosset & Dunlap
A division of Penguin Young Readers Group
345 Hudson Street, New York, New York 10014
First published in Great Britain 2005 by Frederick Warne
as *Spot's Storybook*
Copyright © 2005 by Eric Hill
All rights reserved
Planned and produced by Ventura Publishing Ltd.
80 Strand, London WC2R 0RL, England
Printed in Singapore
ISBN 0-448-43973-5
1   3   5   7   9   10   8   6   4   2

Spot's
Giant Treasury

Eric Hill
Grosset & Dunlap

Contents

Spot's
First
Picnic

Spot was going on his first picnic with his friends Tom, Helen, and Steve, and he was very excited. He squeezed three jam sandwiches into his backpack.
"I hope I haven't forgotten anything," said Spot as he licked his sticky paws.

Then he had an idea.
"Just what we need for our picnic!" shouted Spot.
And before Sally could stop him, Spot had pulled the
tablecloth off the table—and everything with it. *Crash!*

A knock at the door saved Spot from getting into more trouble.

"Your friends are here, Spot," Sally called.

Spot rushed to the door.

"Let's go," said Spot.

"Bye, Mom!"

Sally looked up at the sky. It was cloudy.

"Be careful," she told them. "And come back if it rains."

"Don't worry," said Helen. "I'll be in charge."

They climbed up a hill and Spot pointed to a grassy meadow on the other side.

"Let's go there," he said. "I know where there's a stream and a big tree we can sit under for our picnic. Come on. I'll race you to the stream!"

Spot got there first. Steve was second and Helen came in third. Tom was last, but when he saw the water, he was the first one in. *Splash!*

"It was silly of you to jump in like that, Tom," Helen scolded. "You might have hurt yourself."

"Sorry," said Tom. "But I'm fine now. Let's go and eat."

Spot, Helen, and Steve crossed the stream on stepping stones.

Spot put down the tablecloth and Helen unpacked the food.
They had just started to eat when it began to rain.
"Quick, everyone!" Helen shouted. "Put the tablecloth over
the branch and make a tent."

It was cozy and dry under the tablecloth, but Steve
stayed outside.
"It's only a shower," he said as he climbed up on a branch.
Suddenly Spot heard Steve shout, "Ooops!" and the tent
began to shake. Then everything went dark.

Steve had slipped off the branch and pulled the tent down on top of everyone.

"That's the end of our picnic," moaned Spot.

"It's all your fault, Steve," Helen complained. "You and your silly monkey tricks."

"We may as well go home," said Spot.

They packed up and started back across the stream. But the stones were slippery from the rain and Helen lost her balance.

"Help!" she cried. They all tried to catch Helen, but she fell and pulled everyone into the water with her.

What a mess! Spot looked around and laughed.
"That was your fault, Helen. You and your silly
balancing tricks!"
Everyone started giggling, and Helen laughed too.
"Wait until Mom sees us," Spot said.

But Sally had a surprise ready for them when they got home. "I knew you'd come back wet and hungry so I made you an indoor picnic."
"Thanks, Mom!" said Spot. "We are starving. We didn't mind getting wet at all, but we did mind eating soggy sandwiches!"

Spot
Finds
a Key

Spot was playing in the garden. He saw something shining on the garden path.
"What's that?" he said. "It's a key!"
"Perhaps it's a key to the garden shed," said a bird.

"Let's see," said Spot. He tried to put the key in the lock of the garden shed, but it was too small.

"Dad might know where this key comes from," said Spot. "Here he is. I'll ask him." But Sam was in a hurry. "Sorry, Spot, I can't stop now. I'm looking for something."

"Oh well," said Spot, "I'll try indoors. Perhaps it's the key to Mom's jewelry box."

Spot tried the key in the lock of Sally's jewelry box, but it was too big.
"I'll ask Mom," said Spot. "Mom, do you know what..."
Sally didn't stop to listen. "Sorry, Spot, I must go and help Dad. I'll be back in a minute."

"Perhaps it's the key to the desk,"
thought Spot.
He tried to put the key in the lock of
the desk. The key was the right size,
but it wouldn't turn.

"This game is fun. Where else shall
I try? Perhaps it's the key to the
kitchen cupboard."

He put the key in the lock of the
cupboard. It was the right size and it
turned the lock, but it didn't open
the cupboard.
"Oh," said Spot, disappointed.
"What else can there be? Hmmm,
I wonder why Dad's left his
toolbox on the floor?
Now that's got a lock..."

Spot put the key in the lock of the toolbox.
"It's the right size... and it turns...
and it opens the toolbox!"

"Dad," said Spot. "I've
found the key for the toolbox."
"Well done, Spot," said Sally.
"You are very smart," said Sam,
"because we didn't even tell you
what we were looking for!"

Spot's
Favorite
Toy

Spot and Tom were in the garden playing with Spot's ball. "I think my ball is my favorite toy," said Spot.

Just then it started to rain.
"Let's go inside," said Spot. "Mom, can we play inside?"
"Of course," said Sally. "But you can't play with
the ball inside the house, Spot. You'll have to find
another toy to play with."

Spot and Tom went to Spot's room.
Spot picked up his train.
"Now *this* is my
favorite toy,"
he said.

Tom was looking in the
toy box. He found
Spot's cars.
"Can we play with the
cars, Spot?" he asked.
"They're my favorite."

"Mine too," said Spot. "Come on, let's race them."
Spot's car won the first race, Tom's car won the
second race, and in the third race the cars went
so fast that they hit the dresser with a big bang.
"Be careful, boys!" called Sally.

"I've got to go now," said Tom.
"See you tomorrow, Spot."
Spot was sorry to see Tom leave.

"Now what shall I play with?" thought Spot when Tom had gone.
"I know, my building blocks."

"Helen's here," called Sally.

"Hello, Helen," said Spot. "Help me build a tower with my building blocks. They're my favorite toy."

"Mine too," said Helen. "Let's see how high we can make it."

As Helen placed her block on top, the tower wobbled. Spot tried to hold it. *Crash!* Spot and Helen and the blocks landed on the floor in a heap.

"It's time to go," said Helen. "Bye, Spot."

"It's bath time, Spot," said Sally.

"That's good," said Spot. "I can play with my boat. It's my favorite toy."

"After your bath you must put all your toys away before you go to bed."

So Spot had his bath and put his toys away and went to bed.

"Did you put all your toys away, Spot?" asked Sally.
"Yes, Mom. All except Teddy. He's in bed with me. He really *is* my favorite toy."

Spot's Hospital Visit

"I'm ready!" Spot shouted to Tom and Helen. They were all going to visit Steve, who was in the hospital with a broken leg.

Tom had a ball for Steve, and Helen was taking her doctor's bag and a big bunch of flowers. She was pushing them in her dolls' stroller. Spot had a basket full of fruit.

"These are for Steve," said Spot.

"We'd better hurry or there won't be any left!" said Helen.

At the hospital, they found Steve's room. Steve waved.
"Thank you for coming," he called. "I love visitors,
especially when they bring me presents!"
Spot looked at the cast on Steve's leg.
"Doesn't that hurt?" he asked.
"Not at all," said Steve. "Anyway, it's coming off tomorrow."

"There's writing on your cast," said Spot.
Steve laughed. "Yes, the doctors and nurses have written
their names on my leg."
"I want to write my name," said Spot. So he did, and then
Tom drew a funny face. Helen wrote her name and drew
some flowers and a heart.

Tom was looking at Steve's hospital bed. There was a handle on the side.
"What's this for?" he asked as he started to turn it.
Steve's head and shoulders rose into the air.
"Hey! Look at that!" shouted Tom.

Spot found another handle on the other side of the bed and began turning. Steve's feet went up.
"Be careful!" Steve yelled. "You're not supposed to do that. I might break something else!"

Suddenly the door opened and Nurse Rabbit came in with a wheelchair.

"Here, Steve," she said. "Why don't you take your friends to the playroom?" They went along the corridor.

"Look at all these toys," said Tom.
"I like this train," said Spot.
Helen opened her doctor's bag and took out a green mask and gown.

"Let's play doctor," she said. "You're my patient, Tom."
So Tom sat down and Helen listened to his chest. He began
to laugh and twist around.
"Sit still!" Helen ordered. "You don't laugh and fool around
when a real doctor examines you."
"But you're tickling me," giggled Tom.

"Let's pretend Spot has broken his leg," said Helen.
She unrolled a bandage and wound it around Spot's leg.
"Put Spot in your stroller, Helen!" shouted Steve.
"Tom, look at Spot." But Tom wasn't there.

Helen wheeled Spot into the hall and Steve wheeled himself out in the wheelchair.

"Where can Tom be?" he asked. They went down the corridor calling out Tom's name. But he was nowhere in sight.

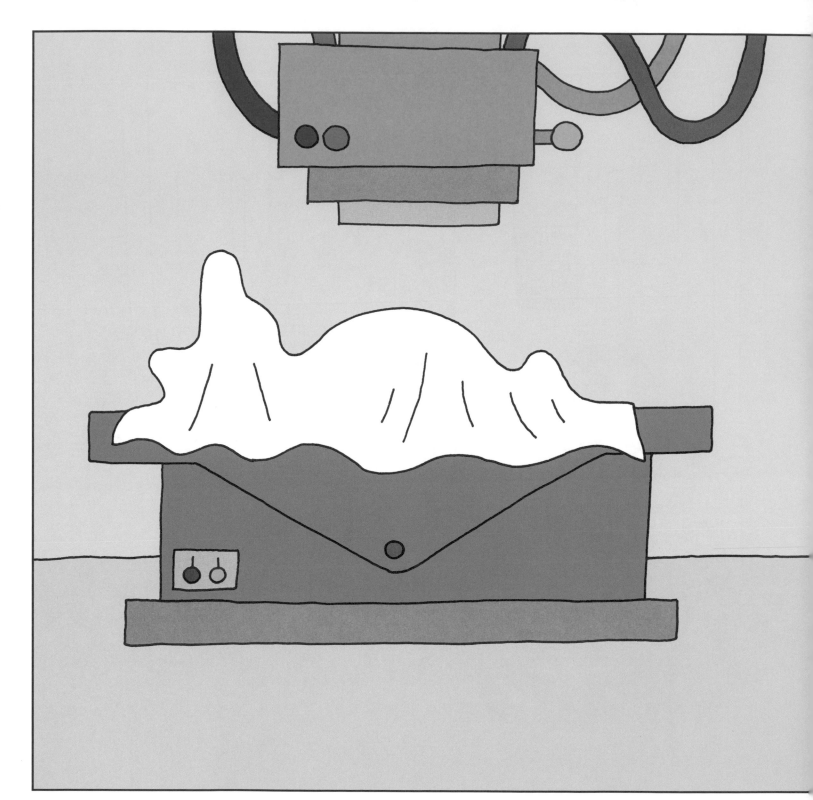

They looked in the X-ray room.
"This is the machine that took pictures
of my leg," Steve told them.
"I know about X-ray machines," said
Helen. "They're like cameras, but they
take pictures of your bones."
"I don't see Tom in here," said Steve.
"Do you?"

As the three friends turned around to leave, a loud voice shouted, "BOO!" They all jumped.
There sat Tom. He'd been hiding under a sheet all the time.
"Did I scare you?" he laughed.

Visiting time was over, so they said good-bye to Steve and went back to Spot's house. Helen wheeled Spot with his bandaged leg all the way in the stroller. Sally was at the door as they arrived.

"Spot!" she cried. "What happened to your leg?"

"Don't worry," Spot told her. "Helen was just playing doctor."

55

"I liked the hospital," said Spot. "We had fun. I think I'd like to be a doctor when I grow up."

"Maybe you will," said Sally. "But in the meantime, Steve will soon be out of the hospital, and you can all play doctor at home."

"Great!" said Spot.

Spot
Goes
Splash!

It was raining when Spot woke up.
"Oh dear," he thought. "I'll have to stay inside. I wonder what Steve and Helen are doing today?"
"Breakfast is ready," Sally called from the kitchen.
Spot loved breakfast. He forgot all about the rain.

After he had finished eating, Spot looked outside again.
"Oh good," he said. "It's stopped raining. Can I go outside and play, Mom?"
"All right," Sally told him. "But don't get all wet and muddy. I've just cleaned the house before Grandma and Grandpa come to visit."

Spot went out into the garden. The sun was beginning to shine. Spot saw Steve looking up at the sky.
"Do you see the rainbow, Spot?" asked Steve.
"Yes!" said Spot. "It's so many different colors."

Helen came along wearing a raincoat, a big rain hat, and shiny red boots.
"It's stopped raining, Helen," said Spot.
"I know," said Helen.

"You don't need your raincoat and hat and boots anymore," Steve told her.

"Yes I do," said Helen, smiling. "Especially the boots. I need them to walk through puddles. Like this…"

And she stomped through a big puddle. *Splash!*

"That looks like fun!" said Spot.
"Let's try it!" said Steve. And they splashed through the puddles too, stomping and shouting.
"You two are silly," said Helen. "Now your feet are all wet and muddy."
"We don't care," they said. "This is great!"

"It's starting to rain again," said Helen. "I'm still nice and dry, and you two will have to go home."
"I suppose so," said Spot, having one last splash.

By the time he got home, Spot was
very wet and very muddy.
Sally was not pleased.
"Get into the bath at once," she said.
"But it's not time to go to bed yet,"
said Spot.
"I know," said Sally, "but it's time
for a bath."

So Spot got into the bath with his boat and toy duck. "This is fun too," he thought. "But now I think I've had enough water for one day."

Spot
at the
Fair

Grandma and Grandpa took Spot to the fair. "What would you like to go on first, Spot?" "I'd like to go on the merry-go-round," said Spot. "Please." Grandpa lifted Spot up onto the horse. "You too, Grandma and Grandpa," said Spot.

"This is fun," Grandpa said. Grandma agreed. "Ooh, I can't remember when I last did this."

"What next, Spot?" asked Grandma.
Spot looked around.
"I'd like to go on the giant slide," he said.

Spot came whizzing down.
"*Wheee!*"
"I'd like to go on that,"
said Grandpa.
"Me too," said Grandma.

Grandma came down the slide followed
by Grandpa.
"This is great, Spot. What a time
we're having!"
Spot laughed to see his grandparents
having so much fun. Then he went down
the slide again.

"Can I go on the bumper cars now?" Spot asked.
"I'll go with you," said Grandma.
"I'll just watch," said Grandpa. A loud buzz started and Spot pushed down on the pedal. They were off.

"There's Helen and Tom! Hold tight, Grandma!" shouted Spot as Helen bumped her car into theirs. *Bang!*
"My word," said Grandma, "this is some ride!"

Then Spot bumped Helen's car.
"That's the fun of it," said Spot, laughing.
Bang!

When the ride finished, Spot and Grandma climbed out of the car.
"That was a little scary," said Grandma.
"It was," said Spot, "but sometimes it's fun to be a little scared."

"Where's Grandpa?" asked Grandma.
He was nowhere in sight.
Suddenly Helen pointed. "I think I can see him.
He's carrying something big and pink."

"Where have you been?" said Grandma. "We were worried."
"I got bored waiting so I tried my luck on the ring toss.
I won this for Spot."
"Wow!" said Spot as he licked the cotton candy Grandpa had
bought for him.
It was time to go.
"Thanks for a great day," said Spot.
"Thank *you*, Spot," said Grandpa. "We enjoyed it
as much as you did."

Sweet Dreams, Spot

It was the start of a busy day. After breakfast, Spot went shopping with his mom. There was a long list of things to get. "Thank you, Spot," said Sally. "I couldn't have done all this without your help."

After lunch, he went to
the park with his dad.
"Come on, Spot," said Sam.
"I'll race you to
the playground."
At the playground, Spot
went on the swings.
"Push me higher, Dad!" said Spot.

When Spot and his dad got home from the park, Helen, Tom, and Steve came over to play hide-and-seek.

Finally, as it was getting dark, Spot's friends went home. Spot was tired from all that playing.

After Spot had eaten his supper, he went
for a last walk in the garden.
"Hello, Spot," a small voice said,
"have you come out to play?"
"No, I'm going to bed," said Spot.
"Oh well," said the mole,
"sleep tight."

As Spot walked by the pond, he heard a frog croak.
"Hello, Spot. It's a lovely evening for a swim."
"Not for me, thanks. I'm ready for bed," said Spot.

"Tu-whit tu-whoo!" hooted the owl.
"Good night, Owl," said Spot.
"What do you mean *good night*?"
the owl asked. "I've just woken up.
I've got lots to do."
"Not me," Spot yawned.
"I've had a busy day already."

Spot went back inside.
"Good night, everyone," he said.
Spot kissed his dad.
"I've had a great day, Dad. Thanks for
taking me to the park."
"Good night, Spot," said Sam.

Sally came in to kiss Spot good night.
"Please read me a story, Mom," said Spot.
Sally opened the book and started to read.

Spot snuggled down.
He got sleepier and sleepier.
By the time the story was
over, Spot was fast asleep.

"What a tired little puppy you were," Sally whispered.
"I've been reading the story and there was no one listening."
"Oh yes there was," said a voice. Sally looked around and
there were the owl, the frog, and the mole.
"Thanks for the story, Sally," they said. "Sweet dreams, Spot."
Spot opened one eye.
"Yes, thanks, Mom," he said.
"Good night, everyone."
And he fell fast asleep again.

Spot's Windy Day

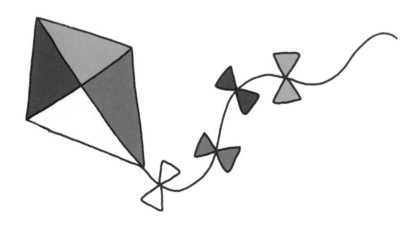

One windy day, Spot went out to fly his kite.
"See you later, Mom," he called to Sally.
"Don't get blown away, Spot!" said Sally.
Spot ran up and down the field with
his kite, trying to get the wind to
lift it up into the air. Suddenly
a strong gust caught the kite.
"Oh!" Spot cried. "Look how high it is!"

Then, "Oops!" said Spot. "How did that happen?" His kite had landed in a tree. Spot looked up at it. "I can't reach up there," he said. "That's the end of flying my kite. Oh no!"

Spot started to walk home. He was a little sad.
Leaves were blowing all around him in the wind.
Red, yellow, green, and orange ones.

"I'll try and catch a leaf," he said. But it was
harder than he thought. As soon as one came
near him, the wind whisked it away again.
Spot looked up and saw something big and dark above him.
"Ooh!" Spot said, reaching up. "What's that?"

It blew here and there. It came lower and lower—and *whoosh*—it landed right on Spot's head and covered his eyes.

Spot couldn't see anything.
But he heard a voice say,
"Well, well, there's my hat!"
Spot pulled on the sides of the hat
and someone pulled on the front.
Pop! Off came the hat and Spot found
himself looking up at Mr. Kangaroo.

"Thank you, Spot. You saved my best Sunday hat!"
"It was nothing," said Spot.
"I wish I could do something for you, Spot!"
said Mr. Kangaroo.
"You can!" said Spot. "My kite is
stuck up in the tree. Can you
reach it?"

"Certainly," said Mr. Kangaroo.
He jumped up and knocked the kite
down to the ground.
"Wow!" said Spot.
"I'm glad your hat
found me!"

Spot's kite once again soared up in the sky.
"Thank you, Mr. Kangaroo!" shouted Spot.
But Mr. Kangaroo couldn't hear.
It was too windy.

Spot
Follows
His Nose

One morning, Spot went out for a walk. He stopped and sniffed.
"What smells so nice?" he asked. Spot went to the flowers in the garden. He sniffed.
"No. That's not what I smell," he said.

His friend Helen came by on her bike.
"Hello, Spot. Why are you sniffing?"
"I smell something really nice," Spot said, "but I don't know
what it is."

"Mr. Kangaroo has just cut his grass,"
said Helen. "Maybe that's what you smell."
Spot ran across to Mr. Kangaroo's house.

"Hey, Spot!" Mr. Kangaroo shouted. "What are you doing in my pile of grass?"
"I was only sniffing at it," said Spot. "But it's not the smell I'm looking for."

Next door, Tom was painting the fence in front of his house.
"I wonder if it's the paint I smell?" said Spot.
He went up to the fence and sniffed.
"That smells awful!"

Tom laughed. "You've got paint on your nose!"
Spot rubbed his nose.
"I have to go home now," he told Tom.

As Spot went up the path to his house, the smell got stronger.
He ran inside. Sally was polishing a table in the hall.
Spot jumped up and sniffed at the tabletop.
"You've put your dirty paws all over my
nice clean table!" cried Sally.
"I'm sorry, Mom," said Spot.
"I've been smelling something nice
all morning. But this isn't it."

"Why don't you look in the kitchen, Spot?"
said Sally.
Spot ran to the kitchen.
"That's the smell!" he shouted.
There on the table was a plate of hot cookies.

"I baked these for later," Sally told him. "But you can have one now." She smiled. "There's nothing wrong with your sense of smell, Spot!"

"No," said Spot. "And there's nothing wrong with my sense of taste either. Thanks for the cookies, Mom!"

a big surprise. Outside,

ot asked.

ur hat and scarf," said
cold outside."

l that, Mom," said Spot,
oor. "Brrr! You're right,
d."

s hat and scarf.

One morning, Spot woke up and got
everything was covered in snow.
"Mom, can I go out with my sled?" S
"Yes, but put on y
Sally. "It's very
"I don't need a
opening the d
Mom. It *is* col
Spot put on hi

By the time Spot had pulled his sled to the top of the hill, he was feeling warm again. He sat on his sled and pushed himself off. *Whoosh!* Down he went to the bottom of the hill. "This is great!" he said.

Steve was skating on the pond.
"Hello, Spot!" Steve called out.
"Do you want to try my skates?"

Skating looked easy when Steve did it. But Spot found it wasn't so easy after all.
"I think I'll stick with my sled. Come and ride with me, Steve."

They climbed the hill, pulling the sled together. When they reached the top they got on the sled.

"Ready, steady... go!"

The sled went much faster with Spot and Steve both on it.

"*Whee!* This is fantastic!" shouted Steve.

"Yes," cried Spot. "Watch out for the... Oh!"

The sled hit a big pile of snow and came to a sudden stop.
Spot and Steve rolled out into the snow.
Then something knocked Spot's hat down over his eyes.
"What's that?" Spot asked.
They heard giggling, and there was Helen, laughing at them all covered in snow.
"It's a snowball," she called. "Here comes another!"
And before he could move, a big, squishy snowball hit Steve in the tummy.

"Watch out!" yelled Steve, throwing a snowball back.
"Here comes another!" shouted Spot.
"Hey!" said Helen. "Two against one isn't fair. Come and help me build a snowman. Look, I've already started."

Helen had rolled a big snowball for the snowman's body.
Spot helped her roll another one for his head.
"Come and help us, Steve," called Spot.
"In a minute," said Steve. "I'm busy."

Helen and Spot put the head on the body. They found two stones for the snowman's eyes and a piece of wood for his mouth.

"Look at our snowman, Steve," called Spot.

"And look at what I've made," said Steve.

Steve had made a "snowdog" on top of Spot's sled.
It looked a lot like Spot.
"That's great!" said Spot. "Why did you build it on my sled?"
"So you could take it home, Spot."
"Mom will be surprised when two Spots come home,"
said Spot. "It's lucky she told me to wear my hat and scarf so she'll know which one is me!"

Spot and His Grandparents Go to the Carnival

Early one morning Spot set off to visit
his grandparents. He said good-bye to
Sally and Sam, and ran to Grandma and
Grandpa's house. Spot was very excited because
it was the day of the carnival, and Grandma and
Grandpa had promised to take him to the big parade.

When he got to the house, Spot rang the doorbell.
Grandpa opened the door. He looked very surprised
to see Spot.
"Hello, Spot!" he said. "What are you doing here?"
"Oh Grandpa!" said Spot. "You're teasing me!
You know we're going to the carnival."
"Of course we are!" said Grandpa, giving
Spot a hug. "Grandma and I have been in the
attic getting things ready.
Come and see."

Spot liked going into the attic. Here Grandma and Grandpa kept all the things that they couldn't fit into the rest of the house. There were chairs and chests, clothes and toys, and pictures and lots and lots of boxes. Grandma was busy sorting out things.

"Hello, Grandma!" said Spot. "Can I help you get ready for the carnival?"

"Why, thank you, Spot," said Grandma.
"My goodness, you're having fun with those boxes.
What have you found under there?"

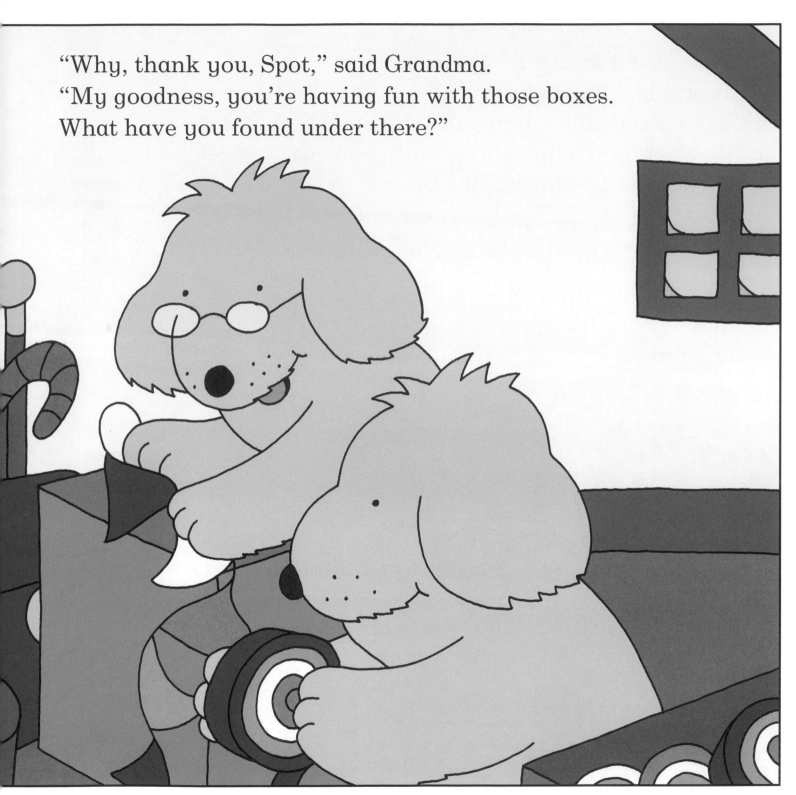

It was an old firefighter's helmet.
"That's mine," said Grandpa.
"Were you really a firefighter, Grandpa?" asked Spot.
"He wasn't just a firefighter," said Grandma.
"He was the Chief Firefighter."
"That reminds me," said Grandpa,
"I've got something to show you."

They went down the stairs and into the
garden. Grandpa made Spot stand next to
the shed and close his eyes. Spot heard
the sound of the shed doors opening
and then an engine starting.
"You can look now, Spot."
said Grandpa.

Spot opened his eyes. In front of him was a
real fire engine with a long ladder
and a big brass bell, and it was
painted bright red.

"Grandpa!" gasped Spot. "Is it really yours?"
"This is the very fire engine I used to work with. The
firefighters have a new one now so I'm looking after this
old one. It just needs a little cleaning before we use it in the
carnival parade."

"The carnival parade! You mean we're going to the carnival on the fire engine? Oh, my friends should see this!"
"But they can come with us, Spot," said Grandpa. "Then we'll have a crew aboard." Grandpa said Spot could go and call his friends right away.

While Spot waited for his friends to arrive, he helped Grandpa clean the fire engine. Grandpa got wet.

Grandpa called out that Helen, Steve, and Tom were here.
There was a wonderful smell coming from the kitchen.
Spot found his friends in the kitchen, eating cookies.

"Your grandma's cookies are fantastic!" said Tom.
"Yes, they are," said Spot. "And what's more, every year she wins the prize for making the best cake at the carnival."

"Come and see Grandpa's fire engine," said Spot.
They all ran to the shed.
"Wow!" said Tom.
"Gosh!" said Helen. Steve just stared.
Grandpa let them climb aboard to try it out.
Spot rang the brass bell.
Ding, ding!

Boom, boom! From somewhere in the distance came an answering echo.
"What was that?" asked Steve.
"Not me," said everyone.
Ding, ding, ding! went Spot with the bell.
Boom, boom, boom! replied the echo.
"It sounds like a drum," said Spot. "Let's go and look." They ran down to the garden gate.

A carnival float was passing by. On the back were three musicians, a bear with a drum, an elephant with a trumpet, and a hippopotamus with a tuba.

"That's my mom!" said Helen. "She plays the tuba in the band. What are you doing, Mom?"

"We're just on our way to collect the rest of the band. Do you want to see our float?"

Tom and Steve liked the musical
instruments. Tom tapped the drum.
It made a very soft *boom, boom.*
Steve blew into the tuba. It made a very loud
SCREECH, SCREECH!
Everyone jumped back and Grandma's cat
ran straight up a tree.

As the float went on
its way, Grandma came out
of the house.
"It's almost time to go to the carnival."
she said. "Have you seen Kitty?"
"She ran up the tree when Steve played
the tuba," said Spot.
Grandma gave Spot a saucer of milk for the cat
and asked him to call her down from the tree.
But the cat didn't come down.

Kitty was sitting on a very high branch. Steve began to climb the tree.
"I'll bring Kitty back down," he said.

A moment later Steve was
sitting on the branch with the cat.
But he didn't come down either.
"I can't carry her. If I am holding her then
I can't climb down the tree. I'll just have to
stay here and keep her company."
"This looks like a job for the Chief Firefighter,"
said Spot, and he ran off to the house.

The red fire engine came bouncing down the path with Grandma at the wheel. It stopped by the tree.
"Quick, put the ladder up, Grandpa!" said Grandma.
"I can't until Spot arrives," said Grandpa. "There's something missing."

And just then Spot came running out of the house with Grandpa's very own helmet.
"There," said Grandpa, putting it on. "Now I'm ready for anything."

Slowly the ladder
rose up to the tree.
As soon as it reached the
high branch, Grandpa climbed
up and rescued Grandma's cat.
Steve came down the ladder
after them. Everyone cheered.
"Well done!" said Grandma.
"Now we can set off for
the carnival."

Ding, ding! They were off.

Suddenly, around the corner, they saw the carnival float parked at the edge of the road.

"Mum," said Helen, "you've got a flat tire."

"We certainly have," said Helen's mom. "How are we going to get to the carnival? Do you have a spare tire?"

"Our spare tire is the wrong size," said Grandpa.
"Is there something we can use instead?"
"I've got an idea," said Spot, and he whispered it in
Grandpa's ear.
"That is a good idea, Spot," said Grandpa.

The band got to the carnival just in time. But they didn't ride on their own float. Thanks to Spot's idea, they joined the carnival parade riding on Grandpa's fire engine.
And what a carnival parade it was!

There were clowns, and jugglers and acrobats, and crowds of people laughing and cheering.

"Look, Grandma! Look, Grandpa! There's Mom and Dad!" shouted Spot. And sure enough, there were Sally and Sam, waving proudly at the fire engine.

Spot waved back and rang the bell as loudly as he could. And just then all the carnival balloons were released at once and it seemed as if the whole parade was covered with shiny falling balloons.

When it was all over, Spot thought it had been the best carnival day ever.

"It was wonderful riding on the fire engine," said Spot.

"And Grandma won the prize for best cake," said Grandpa.

"I think I'll give the prize to Spot this year," said Grandma, "because he saved the day."

Spot took the blue ribbon and pinned it on the wall.

"Let's keep it here with the others," he said. "I think we all saved the day."

Spot
Digs
a Hole

Spot loved to dig holes in his own special garden.
He dug one hole, then another, then another.

Spot then buried something in each hole so that he could have fun finding it again later on.

After his busy day digging holes, Spot was very dirty.
"I think I'll go inside now," said Spot.

Spot's dad was watering the garden. When he saw how dirty Spot was, he said, "You can't go into the house like that, Spot!"
He sprinkled Spot with water from the hose.

"Ooh!" said Spot. "That's great! I'm nice and clean now.
Thanks, Dad!"

Spot went into the house.
"Just in time for your bath,
Spot," said his mom.
"But I'm all clean, Mom,"
said Spot.
Sally looked at the paw marks
on the floor.
"Not clean enough, Spot,"
said Sally.

Spot went up to the bathroom and looked for his toy duck.
"Oh dear," said Spot. "I buried it in a hole this morning..."

Spot ran out to the garden and started to dig.
He found his duck in the third hole.

Spot hurried back to the house with his duck.
He was even dirtier than he had been before.

Spot got into the tub. "Now I really do need a bath," he laughed. "And I can find another toy to hide in the morning."

Spot
Cleans
Up

Spot and Steve had been playing all day and Spot's bedroom was a mess.
"Vroom," said Spot as he pushed a car along the floor.
"Coming in to land!" said Steve, holding an airplane high up in the air.

Spot's mom looked in.

"What a fine time you've had! But it's time to clean up now."

"Okay, Mom," said Spot, with one last push on the car.

"I'll help," said Steve.

Steve put the airplane back in the toy box
with the boat and train set.

All the books went back in the bookcase and the rest of the toys went into the toy box.
"There! All done!" said Spot. "Thanks for your help, Steve."

After Steve had gone home, Spot got ready for bed. "What a fun day I've had," he thought as he brushed his teeth. "*And* I've got a nice clean room."

Spot was just about to climb into his basket
when he noticed something was missing.
He looked around the room.
"Where's Teddy?"

Spot ran to his toy box. One by one, he sorted through the toys. Teddy wasn't there.

Spot went to the bookcase. Maybe Teddy was hidden behind a book? But he wasn't. Spot looked all over. No Teddy.

Sally came in to say good night. "I thought you had cleaned up your room, Spot," she said.
"I did, Mom, but I can't find my Teddy," said Spot.
"I'll help you," said Sally. "Have you looked in your basket?"

Spot rushed to his basket and lifted the cushion.
"I've found Teddy! Thanks, Mom. I promise to clean up again
in the morning."
"I know you will," smiled Sally.
She tucked Spot up with Teddy and whispered,
"Good night, Spot. Good night, Teddy. Sweet dreams."

Spot
Plays
Hide-and-Seek

Spot was playing in his bedroom when he had an idea.
"I want to play hide-and-seek," he said. He took all the toys
out of his toy box and climbed inside. After a moment,
Spot looked out.
"I need someone to find me," he said.
Spot climbed out and
ran downstairs.

Spot's mom was in the kitchen as Spot ran by. He saw
a laundry basket.
"Ah, that's a good place to hide," he said.
He jumped in just as Sally walked past.

"Boo!" said Spot.
Sally turned around and laughed.
"I didn't see you, Spot," she said.
"Good. Will you play hide-and-seek with me?" asked Spot.
"All right," said Sally. "We can play in the garden."

"I'm playing hide-and-seek with my mom," said Spot
to the rabbit.
"You're too big to hide in here," said the rabbit.

Sally looked behind the bushes.
She looked in the vegetable patch.

180

She looked over the wall.
"Where can Spot be hiding?" said Sally.
"Not here," said the goose.

Spot heard Sally coming.
"Hide behind the tree," said the
squirrel. "I won't tell."

Sally walked past the tree and went to the shed.
"Look out, Spot," she called,
"I'm coming to find you."

Spot wasn't in the shed.
"I don't know where Spot can be,"
said Sally. "Perhaps he has gone
back to the house to hide."

Spot's dad came along and picked up the wheelbarrow.
"Have you seen Spot?" asked Sally.
"No," said Sam.

"Hi, Dad," said Spot, standing up.
"I've been hiding from Mom."
"Yes, Spot, I know," said Sam.
"She has gone back to the house
to look for you."

"I think I've done enough hiding," said Spot.
"I'll go back too." As he got to the house,
Spot heard his mom call out, "Steve is here,
Spot. He wants to play."

"Hello, Spot," said Steve. "Do you want to play hide-and-seek?" Spot thought for a moment.
"Okay," said Spot, "but only if you hide and I seek."
"Great," said Steve.

Spot started to count as Steve ran off
to hide.
"Good luck, Steve," said Sally.
"If Spot seeks as well as he hides,
it will be a short game!"